A Grim Pet

∞ ∞ ∞ ∞ ∞

M.K. Eidem

The Imperial Series

Cassandra's Challenge

Victoria's Challenge

Jacinda's Challenge

Tornians

Grim

A Grim Holiday

Wray

Oryon

Ynyr

A Grim Pet

Kaliszians

Nikhil

Treyvon

Kiss

Kirall's Kiss

Published by Turtle Point Publishing
Copyright © 2018 by Michelle K. Eidem
Cover Design by Judy Bullard
Edited by: azedit@southslope.net

Chapter One

Lisa just smiled as Grim, for the third time, checked to make sure her cape was securely closed against the slight chill in the air before doing the same to the girls'. The capes weren't the same gray ones they had worn at the Joining Ceremony. Grim had those destroyed, never wanting to be reminded of how he nearly lost his family. Now they wore capes in the deep, purple color of his house, House Luanda.

"We are fine, Grim," Lisa told him as he went to adjust her hood again. "It's not that cold out."

"I should have considered that the sun would not have yet warmed this area when I chose it," he grumbled.

"But it will soon," she said, putting a reassuring hand over his. "I can't believe you and your Warriors were able to get all this done in such a short time."

She let her gaze travel over the newly-constructed, circular arena that now sat on the grounds in front of House Luanda. There was a raised seating area that curved around half of it, and then a gathering area for Warriors at the far end. Today was the Festival of the Goddess, but it wasn't like any festival Lisa had ever experienced back on Earth.

For Tornians, the Festival was a competition. A way for them to impress the Goddess with their strength and skill, in the hopes she would find them fit and worthy enough to bless them with a female. It was armed combat, and it wasn't uncommon for Warriors to be injured, sometimes severely.

Lisa had been horrified when Grim informed her of this and told him that there was no way she could allow the girls to witness such a thing. It would terrify them to watch Warriors, that they had come to know and love, attacking and injuring one another.

They had finally reached a compromise, and in a short time, they would discover if Grim's Warriors would accept it.

"They knew it was their Queen's wish, so it was done," Grim told her, referring to the arena as if it shouldn't surprise her.

"They are all fit and worthy males," Lisa said, smiling up at him, "but I got the best of them."

"I should never have let you out of our chambers this morning," Grim growled as he leaned down, capturing her lips in a long, deep kiss, his hands slipping under the cape he'd just taken so much time to make sure was closed. He was about to lift her up into his arms and carry her away, when he heard Alger clearing his throat, and the girls starting to giggle.

Pulling his mouth from his Lisa's, he almost ignored them all when the look in her eyes told him she wanted that too. Instead, he took a deep breath and forced himself to release her, only standing after he made sure her cape was secure again.

"Go," she encouraged softly. "We'll finish this tonight."

Giving her a stiff nod, he turned and stepped to the front of the podium to address the large crowd that had gathered. Traditionally, the Warriors that wished to compete would gather at the training fields, but Lisa had expanded the Festival into a daylong event. She had invited vendors from every corner of Luda to set up within the walls of the House and offer their food, wares, and skills for credits. When they quieted, Grim spoke.

"Warriors, today is the Festival of the Goddess." A roar of excitement went through the crowd, and Grim raised his hands to quiet them. "And we must give thanks for the many blessings she has bestowed on us." He turned and looked to Lisa, Carly, and Miki as a roar of agreement spread through the crowd.

"These blessings have changed our lives for the better," Grim continued once they quieted again. "Now, we must show the Goddess that we appreciate them." A confused silence met this statement. "As Warriors, we are used to the blood and gore that comes with battle. We must accept it. But Queen Lisa, Princesses Carly and Miki, and every other female here today do not. And I, for one, never want them to."

A low murmur of agreement answered him.

"Because of this, our battle swords and blades will not be used during the competition. Instead, only stingers shall be allowed." He gestured to the array of stingers propped up against the platform below him. "Any Warrior receiving three stings shall be deemed defeated."

Absolute silence met Grim's declaration, and Lisa let her concerned gaze travel over those before them. Had she overstepped in asking this of Grim? Rising, she went to stand beside him.

"I realize this comes as a shock to you," she said taking Grim's hand. "You believe that only by pitting your full strength and skill against your brother Warriors will you prove to the Goddess you are fit and worthy males." She let her words hang there for a moment, and saw many of the Warriors nodding their heads. "I do not believe that is truth. I do not believe that winning one competition is enough to prove you are a fit and worthy male." She saw they didn't understand.

"Was Faber not once a winner?" she asked, knowing he was. "Was he a fit and worthy Warrior?"

"No." Came the immediate reply.

"Luuken once won in his manno's House. Was he a fit and worthy warrior?" she demanded.

"No!" They shouted even louder.

"Then I say to you that while winning this competition allows others to see the strength and skills you have acquired through your dedication and sacrifice, it has absolutely nothing to do with you being a fit and worthy Warrior. It is your everyday actions that the Goddess sees, and that is what she blesses."

"If you share this belief, then from now on the victor in the Festival of Goddess competition shall receive a trophy created by Master Glassmaker Gahan, and credits equal to a Warrior's yearly compensation." A murmur of excitement went through the crowd, and Lisa raised a hand to quiet them. "Or if you do not share this belief, then you may continue the competition as it has always been with your battle swords and blades, but the Princesses and I shall not witness it. We have no desire to watch the fit and worthy males we have come to care about senselessly harming one another. The choice is yours."

Lisa stood beside Grim, silently waiting to see what the Warriors before her would decide when out of the corner of her eye she caught Alger beginning to move.

"Stay," Grim growled lowly, and Alger stilled.

Both the King's and Queen's Guard had elected not to participate in today's events. Instead, they surrounded the area where Grim and Lisa sat with the females from Earth, along with Padma, Gossamer, Gahan, Dagan, and Caitir.

Because of this, Grim was not going to let The Guard influence the others now. It would be his Warriors' decision on how they proceeded. Slowly, Warrior Tagma separated himself from the group of Warriors on the far side of the arena and moved toward his King and Queen, his battle sword strapped to his back.

Once he stood in front of them, he placed his arm across his chest and gave them a deep bow. Straightening, he released the clasp that held his sword in place and wrapped the now loose straps around the sheath-encased blade. Setting it against the wall beneath where Lisa and Grim stood, he chose the stinger that best fit his grip. Turning, he walked to the center of the arena and waited.

It didn't take long for Warrior Oya to step forward. He exchanged his weapon, took up his position across from Tagma, and saluting him with the stinger he had chosen, waited for the command.

"Begin!" Grim roared, and with a cheer from the crowd, the Festival began.

Lisa blinked back the tears that wanted to fill her eyes as she sat down. She should have had more faith in the Warriors of Luda. Should have known they would understand and be willing to change. They truly were fit and worthy males.

"My Lisa?" Grim asked quietly, concern-filled eyes looking down at her.

"I'm fine," she reassured, giving him a watery smile. "It's just hormones."

"Hormones?" He frowned at the word.

"Chemicals that are naturally in our bodies," she explained. "They increase when a female conceives. It tends to make us just a little," Lisa lifted her hand so he could see that her thumb and index finger were just barely apart, "emotional."

"I will find Hadar! He will fix this." Lisa's hand on his arm stopped him.

"No, Grim. There's nothing he can do about this. It's normal. Natural. It isn't harmful."

"Truth?"

"Truth. I was just touched that our Warriors would so readily accept this change." She had to take a deep breath to fight the new swell of tears. She knew if she didn't, Grim would be carrying her back inside Luanda.

"Mommy?" Carly's little voice had her looking down to see the eyes of her oldest locked on the two Warriors in the arena.

"Yes, baby?"

"Why is that Warrior attacking Cook?"

"Oya isn't attacking Tagma, Carly. We talked about this. Remember? They are just competing against one another."

"But it looks like he is."

"I know, but they aren't using real swords. See?" Lisa pointed to Tagma's and Oya's swords that had just clashed and the flashes of light sparked from them. "They are using stingers."

"But it still hurts," Carly argued when Tagma growled out as Oya's stinger connected with his arm.

"It does, my Carly," Grim took over the conversation, not downplaying what she was seeing. "But it is a way for a Warrior to learn and improve his skills so that when it *is* real, he won't be harmed."

"Oh." Carly was silent for a moment then her gaze went to Grim. "I still don't like it, Manno."

Grim felt his heart stutter. It had been just that morning that Carly and Miki had asked if they could call him Manno instead of Grim, and he knew it would be a long time before hearing it didn't affect him.

"That is good, my Carly. It shows the Warriors that you truly care for their well-being. Just as your mother does."

Carly's little chest puffed up at her manno's praise. It reminded Grim that it was the little things he did that truly affected those he loved. A roar from the Warriors had both Grim's and Carly's attention returning to the arena to find Tagma with three marks on his arms and Oya with only two; declaring the Captain of the Castle Guard the victor.

"Can I go make sure that Cook is okay?" Carly asked, looking back to her manno.

"Yes, Ion and Nairn will escort you." The two guards he named immediately moved to the steps.

∞ ∞ ∞ ∞ ∞

Oya grunted his thanks as he took the cloth Tagma held out, and wiped away the sweat and dirt from their battle.

"It was a good match, old friend."

"It was," Tagma agreed. "I will make sure I spend more time on the fields before we meet at the next Festival."

"It will not change the result," Oya declared. "Your time in the kitchen has dulled your skills."

"As if walking a wall has sharpened yours," Tagma fired back.

"I am not the one out of the competition," Oya told him smugly. "If you wish great rewards, you must prove you are worthy."

"Cook!" The young voice had both Warriors quickly spinning around to find Princess Carly rushing toward them, two of the Queen's Elite Guard closely following.

"Princess Carly," Tagma frowned at Ion and Nairn, even as he went down on one knee, so he was closer to her level. "This is no place for you."

"I had to make sure you were okay. Manno said you were, but..." She reached out a little hand but didn't touch the red slashes that marred his arm and chest, courtesy of Oya's stinger.

"King... your manno," Tagma corrected himself, his eyes widening slightly at how she referred to Grim, "is right. These will be gone by tomorrow."

"Truth?" Her amber gaze searched his.

"Truth, little one. You will see that for yourself when you come help me with the cookies tomorrow."

Carly was silent for a moment, and all the males surrounding them could see she was thinking.

"Alright, but I want to make sure," she said, and before anyone knew what she was about, she leaned forward and pressed a little kiss to each red slash. "Whenever I get hurt, Mommy kisses my boo-boos, and it makes them feel better. Did I make yours feel better, Cook?"

Tagma's breath caught for a moment, and he knew that even if he were in the most excruciating of pain, he would still tell her she'd made it better. "You did, little one," he told her gruffly. "Thank you."

The smile she gifted him with shone brighter than the Tornian sun. "Good. I'll see you tomorrow then." And with that, and a little wave, she was gone.

Slowly rising, Tagma looked to Oya. "I believe I just received a greater reward than you could ever receive in the arena."

"Truth," Oya agreed quietly.

∞ ∞ ∞ ∞ ∞

Lisa moved from stall to stall talking to the vendors, perusing what they had to offer. There were small bits of things she couldn't identify. Handmade jewelry. Woven baskets. And of course, there were blades and swords in every shape and size. Seeing them made her conscious of the Raptor's Claw strapped to her arm. Grim had insisted she carry it. It didn't matter that she was surrounded by her Elite Guard. She carried his offspring, and he was taking no chances.

She couldn't help but smile as she rubbed the pronounced baby bump she already sported. Grim's unborn daughter was making her presence known, making Lisa look more like she was five months pregnant, instead of the three that she was.

She knew it concerned Grim. Her rapidly growing size. He worried that conceiving his offspring would harm her, but Lisa wasn't. Yes, Tornian offspring were larger than human ones at birth, or presentation as they referred to it. And yes, the length of the pregnancy was a month shorter, but Hadar and Rebecca were constantly monitoring her, and she was feeling fine.

"Mommy, can we go see if Dagan wants to play in the garden?" Miki asked, looking up at her hopefully.

Looking a little farther down the path, Lisa saw Padma with Gossamer and Dagan at her side. They had all left the arena together during the break between rounds but had gotten separated as they wandered through the stalls.

"You don't want to watch more of the tournament?" When the girls just looked at each other, Lisa frowned. "Girls?"

"We don't like seeing them fight, Mommy," Carly whispered looking up at her with regretful eyes. "I know Manno said they aren't *really* being hurt, but they still *are* being hurt."

"I see."

"Will Manno be mad?" Miki asked.

"Mad about what?" Grim asked coming up behind them. He didn't like the way his girls jumped at his question or the guilty looks they gave him. He looked questioningly at Lisa. "My Lisa?"

"The girls were just asking if they and Dagan could go play in the garden."

Grim frowned at that, his mind going over the security issues involved. The Festival was being held on the grounds between the front entrance of House Luanda and the gate, making it easily defendable with guards stationed along the walls. The gardens his girls liked to play in were behind the House. While there were guards there, there weren't as many.

"Please, Manno?" Miki asked, and two sets of little eyes pleaded with his. Grim felt his heart melt. There was little he could deny them when his girls looked at him like that.

"You will take Ion, Nairn, and Caius with you," he finally agreed, and the guards named stepped forward.

"We will, Manno!" they squealed, jumping up and down.

"And you will *obey* them," he growled as he went down on a knee to give each of them a hug.

"We will, Manno. Truth," they promised, each kissing a cheek. With that, they went running toward Dagan, their guards running to keep up.

"It seems you were right again, my Lisa," Grim said, his gaze finally leaving the girls.

"Only because I've been a parent longer than you. One day they are going to want to watch, and that's when *you* aren't going to want them to."

"Why would I not want them to?" Grim questioned, frowning at her.

"Because that's when they are going to be watching the Warriors as a female watches a male."

"No!" Grim's denial was loud and had heads turning in their direction. "That will not happen. No male will ever be fit or worthy enough for our girls."

"I think that will be up to them to decide." Lisa hid her smile at Grim's reaction by linking her arm through his so they could walk. "But it will be a long time before you will need to worry about that."

"A *very* long time," Grim agreed.

Chapter Two

"Come on, Dagan!" Miki shouted running passed where he had stopped on the garden path. "Carly is nearly to the rock."

Miki was the youngest and smallest of the three. Because of that, she never got anywhere first, but she tried. Now she was gaining on Carly, but when she looked back to see how close Dagan was, she found he was still at the tree but on his knees now.

Slowing, she turned then headed back to him. "Dagan? What's wrong?"

"There is something in there," he said leaning forward to peer between the full, low-hanging branches that touched the ground.

"There is?" she questioned as she dropped down beside him. "What?"

"I do not know, but I heard it."

"What are you looking at?" Carly asked, coming up behind them.

"Dagan says there's something in our tree," Miki told her sister, her gaze never leaving the tree.

"Really?" Carly dropped down beside them. "What?"

"I do not know," Dagan repeated. "But..."

Just then, a short, sharp screech came from beneath the tree causing all three of them to fall back on their butts.

"There... there *is* something under there," Miki whispered and quickly flipping over onto her hands and knees crawled closer to the tree.

"Miki, get back," Carly told her. "You don't know what it is."

"Whatever it is, it is in pain. It's afraid," Dagan said.

"How can you tell?" Carly asked looking to Dagan.

"I just can," he said, shrugging his shoulders.

"Then we need to help it," Miki said, crawling under the branches.

"Miki!" Carly tried to grab her sister's ankle, but Miki was too fast for her.

"Come on, you two, it's awesome under here."

Dagan and Carly looked at each other. Miki was always doing this. She would just take off and expect them to follow. It had gotten them all in trouble more than once.

"We cannot let her be in there alone," Dagan told her.

"I know," Carly sighed. Sometimes she hated being the older sister. "Let's go."

Together they crawled beneath the bottom limbs and were shocked at what they discovered. The low branches outside actually attached to the tree several feet up, leaving a large, open area that was like a private world meant just for them.

"Wow..." Carly whispered as she looked around.

"I told you," Miki said smugly.

"Look," Dagan said, and their gazes traveled to where he pointed at the dark form near the trunk of the tree.

Suddenly, what had appeared to be a small, non-threatening mass, rose and grew until it was nearly as tall as Miki. It spread its wings, and it let out a screech that had them covering their ears and looking at it in shock.

"It's a raptor," Carly whispered, her voice full of awe.

"He is hurt." Dagan pointed to how the tip of one of the raptor's wings hung down.

"But he can't be hurt," Miki cried out in distress. "He's the Great Raptor. Who is going to protect us now?"

The bird tipped its head to the side, its purple gaze staring at Miki as if it understood her words. Slowly, it folded its wings back into its sides.

"He can't be the Great Raptor, Miki," Carly told her. "He's not big enough. Manno said he was so big that he could block the sun."

"Truth," Miki murmured, "but then maybe he's the Great Raptor's son."

"Manno never said that in any of his stories."

"Maybe he just hasn't gotten to that story yet," Miki stuck her chin out stubbornly at her sister. "He said he had thousands of stories still to tell us."

"Truth." Carly had to agree with her sister.

"How do we help him?" Miki looked to Dagan.

"I do not know for sure," Dagan said slowly, his head leaning to the side just like the raptor's. "I have never cared for a raptor before."

"But you have cared for other animals, right?" Miki demanded. "You told us how you healed a kepie."

"Yes, but that is a much smaller bird."

"So healing a bigger one should be easier," Miki told him.

"All I did was keep it warm and make sure it had food and water. The rest it did itself."

"Oh," Miki frowned at that. "Well then, that's what we'll do for Prince."

"Prince?" Both Dagan and Carly asked.

"Well that's what he is, isn't he, if he's the Great Raptor's son? The Great Raptor protects Luda just like Manno does, and Manno is a King. So the Great Raptor is a King. And his son is a Prince, just like we are Princesses."

Dagan and Carly found themselves slowly nodding at Miki's three-year-old logic, and it seemed the raptor liked it too, as he gave a low caw and then settled back down onto the ground, its injured wing sticking out slightly. Its piercing eyes were just about to close when a call from Ion had them shooting back open.

"Princess Miki! Princess Carly!" Ion shouted, his quick steps followed by Nairn's and Caius'. "Where are you?"

"We need to go, Miki," Carly whispered, peeking between the branches once their guards had passed.

"But what about Prince?"

"He will be fine here, Miki," Dagan told her. "It is why he chose this location."

"But... he needs food and water, and look," she pointed, and they all saw a shiver go through his black body. "He's cold."

"We'll come back with those, but we have to *go,* Miki. Otherwise, Ion will tell Manno we didn't obey him, and then we *won't* be able to come see Prince."

"Oh, all right," Miki grumbled, obviously not happy but agreeing. But as they started to crawl back out, she stopped and looked at the shivering raptor. Slipping off her cape, she crawled toward the deadly creature. "Here, take this. Padma made me another one."

Carefully she draped the cape over the bird, not noticing how close she was to its sharp, deadly beak. "I'll be back as soon as I can with food and water. You just rest and try to get better." With that, she crawled out from under the tree.

∞ ∞ ∞ ∞ ∞

"Miki," Lisa waited until the gaze of her youngest rose from the dinner plate to her. Both girls had been unusually quiet during the meal. "Ion says you lost your cape today. How?"

"I... umm..." Miki's gaze went to Carly before returning to her mother. She'd never lied to her mother before. Well, not really. She didn't count saying she'd only had two cookies when she'd actually had three. But this... "I took it off so I could explore one of the trees and forgot to put it back on."

"But it was cold out," Grim said frowning at her.

"It wasn't that bad, Manno."

"I'm disappointed in you, Miki Renee," Lisa told her. "Padma worked very hard on creating that cape for you, and you just left it?"

"I'm sorry, Mommy." Miki's little eyes filled with tears as she looked at her mother.

"Tomorrow we will go into the garden and find your cape."

"Yes, Mommy."

"Now finish eating." She looked to Carly seeing she had hardly eaten anything either. "Both of you. Then go get ready for bed."

"Yes, Mommy," they said together.

They both quickly finished their meal, then as they rose, Miki paused beside Grim. "Will you tell us another story about the Great Raptor, Manno?"

"I will, once you are in bed," Grim told her wondering why she was asking. He always told them a story, but before he could ask, they were gone.

"They're up to something," Lisa said watching the girls hurry out of the room whispering to each other.

"What could they be up to?" Grim asked frowning. "They had guards with them all day."

"Then where were they when Miki took off her cape?"

"I..." Grim realized she was right. That shouldn't have been possible. "You are right. I will find better Warriors to guard our girls."

"Grim, no, that's not what I meant. Ion and Nairn are the perfect guards for the girls." She instantly defended the two Warriors. They had more than proven themselves in her eyes with how they sacrificed themselves so she and the girls could get away when Luuken had tried to take them. "They give them the space they need to play and explore, to be little girls, while still protecting them. What I was trying to say, and apparently not doing a very good job of it, is that our girls are smart and if they wanted to keep something from us they could."

"You think that is what they are doing?"

"Yes."

"Then I will go get them to tell us what it is." Grim stood, meaning to go after his girls.

"No, Grim."

"No?" He turned to frown at her. "What do you mean? They shouldn't be keeping things from us. What if it is something that harms them?"

"Are you telling me you never kept things from your manno growing up?"

"I..." Grim's cheeks darkened. "Yes, but that is different."

"Really?" Lisa smiled as she rose and stepped into his waiting arms. "Why?"

"Because I'm male, and they are female," he told her gruffly, enfolding her in his arms.

"Really?" Lisa leaned back in his arms giving him a teasing look. "*That's* the reason you're giving me? Because you're male?"

"Females..."

"Have as much right to do what they want as any male does."

"They need to be protected," he argued.

"Truth," she agreed. "But doing one doesn't mean you can't do the other. They need to explore, Grim. Need to find their place in this world. And they can't do that if you lock them away. If you don't give them some freedom. The garden is a safe place."

"It wasn't for you," he growled, remembering Luuken.

"And that will never happen again. Not only because Wray recognized me as your Queen, but because you have tripled the guards along that portion of the wall." She reached up to gently cup his cheek. She knew it still bothered him that she was attacked in their garden. "We are safe there, Grim. Because of you."

"You mean everything to me, my Lisa. You, our girls, and the one yet to come." He reached down running a careful hand over her protruding stomach.

Lisa couldn't help but smile. Grim loved her changing shape. He was always touching and caressing her, especially her belly. He still couldn't seem to believe that *his* offspring was growing there.

"And you mean everything to us."

"Manno!" The girls' little voices called from their room. "We're ready for our story."

"And it seems the ones we currently have are impatient for their story."

"Yes, they always are." He smiled slightly at that. "So we let them keep their secret?"

"For now, yes. They won't be able to keep it to themselves for long," she told him, and together they went to their girls.

∞ ∞ ∞ ∞ ∞

"Manno?"

"Yes, my Miki?" Grim asked, sitting down beside her on the bed she shared with her sister.

"Can you tell us a story about the Great Raptor's son?"

"His what?" Grim looked at Lisa, who was on the other side of the bed next to Carly and frowned.

"Male offspring," Lisa supplied. There were still times when Earth words slipped into their conversations that Grim didn't understand.

"Oh." He looked back to Miki. "Why would you think he had a son, Miki?"

"Well he would have to... wouldn't he? You have mommy and us. The Great Raptor must have a family too."

"I..." Grim realized that in all his existence it was something he had never considered. The Great Raptor just was. But looking at the expectation in his daughters' eyes, he knew he couldn't disappoint them.

"The Great Raptor's son helps him guard the skies of Luda...."

∞ ∞ ∞ ∞ ∞

Lisa released a tired sigh as she rested her head on Grim's chest with a leg thrown over his, her hand resting over his heart, as her rounded stomach nestled against his flat one. Grim pulled her close, his hand gently caressing her belly.

"You did too much today," he growled gruffly.

"Not too much," she denied. "I didn't meet with Ull, as we planned, but it was a long day."

"You will see him and those with him tomorrow."

"With him?" She tilted her head up to look at him. "I thought it was just Ull I was meeting with."

"So did I, but it seems there is a Kaliszian ship traveling with him."

"Why? Because of the Ganglian ship the Kaliszians found with Earth females?"

"Yes, that is my belief."

"Then we need to get up and meet with them." Lisa started to rise, only to have Grim's arm tighten, stilling her.

"Ull has already gone back to the Searcher. He and the others will return tomorrow after you have rested."

"Oh." She laid her head back down and snuggled in closer, silently glad she didn't have to get out of bed. "You did a wonderful job coming up with that story about the Great Raptor's son."

"It was that obvious?"

"Only to me."

"They continually surprise me with their questions."

"They make you look at things differently, don't they?"

"They do," he agreed, reaching up to touch the blue and green thumbprints attached to the necklace the girls had given him just that morning, and how they requested to call him Manno.

Lisa covered his hand with hers, knowing what he was thinking. "They love you very much, Grim. So do I."

"I know," he told her gruffly, his fingers tightening on hers. "It makes me the most blessed male in all the universes, Known or Unknown. Now rest, my Lisa."

Chapter Three

"Eat up, girls," Lisa told her daughters the next morning. "Once you're done, we are going to go find the cape you forgot in the garden yesterday."

"Yes, Mommy," they said, but Lisa caught the look they gave each other. Yes, there was definitely something going on that they didn't want Grim or her to know about. She'd have to keep a close eye on them.

"Lisa." Grim walked back into their room. He'd left a few moments ago to take a comm. "Ull and the others have transported down. They are waiting for us in my Command Room."

"Already?"

"Yes, it seems General Rayner wants to get back to Pontus as soon as possible."

"General Rayner?"

"He is the Supreme Commander of Kaliszian Defenses," Grim informed her. "The other ship traveling with the Searcher is his. He also has his True Mate with him."

"True Mate?"

"I forget you have not met a Kaliszian yet."

"No, I haven't, but Kim told me about the one that gave her a blade."

"Yes, that was General Rayner."

"It saved her life on Vesta. I would very much like to meet the male that defied Wray and gave her that blade."

Grim's lips tightened as he remembered Wray telling him exactly what had happened between him and the General. Had the General not backed down, the two Empires might now be at war, something neither wanted. They needed each other too much.

"Rayner is not a male you wish for an enemy," he told her. "That he has his True Mate with him is surprising though."

"Why? Do the Kaliszians hide away their True Mates the way you Tornians do your females?"

"No, there is no reason for them to. While Kaliszians have more than enough females, they haven't had True Mates since the Great Infection struck."

"You mean besides taking away their ability to feed their people, the Great Infection also took away the Kaliszians' ability to find true love?"

"Yes."

"That seems doubly harsh."

"Two were harmed, my Lisa," he gently reminded her, his gaze going to Carly and Miki. He had always believed he understood the horror of what Emperor Berto had done to his young females. But now, looking down at his daughters gazing up at him with so much love and trust in their little eyes, the true horror of it hit and sickened him. That type of betrayal was so unthinkable to him, so evil. If any male even *thought* about his girls that way, he would end them. Painfully.

"Grim?" Lisa asked quietly, pulling his attention from the girls. She didn't like how hard his eyes had gotten or how his skin had darkened. She'd only seen him look this way once before, and that had been after Luuken had attacked her. Looking back to her daughters, she realized what had him so upset, the thought of *their* daughters being abused that way. "It will never happen, Grim. You would never allow anyone to harm them."

"It wasn't *anyone*, Lisa," he murmured, looking at her.

"No, it wasn't. But that is something *you* would never do." Reaching for his hand, she rested it on her stomach. "To any of our offspring."

"I wouldn't, my Lisa." His hand curved protectively over her stomach. "My vow."

"I know." Stretching up on her toes, she gently kissed his lips.

"Sire." They turned to find Alger standing in the doorway. "Warrior Ull and General Rayner are waiting."

"We will be right there, Alger."

"Yes, sire," Alger bowed slightly to Lisa then left the room.

"Girls." Lisa looked to them. "Your manno and I need to go meet with some people. Ion and Nairn will stay with you."

"Can they take us out into the garden so we can find my cape?" Miki asked.

Lisa frowned. When she had informed the girls that directly after first meal they would be going to find the forgotten cape, neither had been enthusiastic.

"You want to go find your cape?"

"Yes, Mommy," Miki told her.

"Alright. Ion and Nairn can take you."

∞ ∞ ∞ ∞ ∞

Looking over their shoulders to make sure Ion and Nairn weren't watching, Carly and Miki quickly scooted under the branches where the raptor rested.

"Hi, Prince. We're back," Miki said moving toward the bird that was snuggled down in the nest he had made out of her cape. "Are you feeling better?"

Unfazed that the raptor just continued to look at her, she continued. "We brought you something to eat."

That had Prince lifting his head, his purple eyes zeroing in on the strips of rashtar she was pulling from her pocket. She'd managed to slip them into her pocket at first meal while her mom and manno were talking. Sitting down in front of him, she broke off a piece and held it out to him.

"Be careful, Miki," Carly said, being the protective sister she always was.

"He won't hurt us, Carly," Miki told her with all the confidence of a three-year-old. "We're helping him."

As the girls talked, the raptor rose from his warm nest until he towered over them. Slowly, he lowered his deadly beak and carefully snatched the food from her hand.

"See," Miki said to her sister smugly. "I told you he wouldn't hurt us."

∞ ∞ ∞ ∞ ∞

Lisa made no comment when Grim stepped in front of her, pausing for a moment as he opened the doors to his Command Room. She knew why he was doing it. Even though Ull and General Rayner were considered worthy males, Grim would take no chances with her and their unborn daughter's safety. After several tense moments, he moved to the side and put a protective hand on the small of her back, guiding her into the room.

Beside Alger and Agee, there were three other people in the room. One was the warrior she knew as Ull. Standing a few steps away from him was a massive male with beads in his hair, and behind him was a small, cloaked figure.

"Warrior Ull," Lisa acknowledged, her cool gaze running over him. She still wasn't sure he was the right person for this task, but she would give him the benefit of the doubt since Grim and Wray seemed to think he was.

After a moment, that dragged out long enough for Grim to start growling his displeasure, Ull bowed slightly. "Majesty."

Grim gave Ull a hard look before he led Lisa toward the other male. "Lisa, this is General Treyvon Rayner, Supreme Commander of Kaliszian Defenses. General Rayner, my Queen, Lisa Vasteri."

"Majesty, it is a great honor to meet you." Treyvon crossed an arm over his chest and gave her a much deeper bow than Ull had. "May I present to you my True Mate, Jennifer Rayner."

The cloaked figure stepped forward, and when the cape's hood lowered, Lisa gasped. "You're from Earth!"

"I am," Jen affirmed.

"But... What? How? I just assumed you'd be Kaliszian." She turned to face Grim. "You didn't tell me she was from Earth."

"I did not know," Grim told her, frowning darkly at the General.

"It was felt that the fewer Tornians who know there were Earth females in the Kaliszian Empire, and that they could be our True Mates, the better." Treyvon ran hard eyes to the guards in the room.

"That is truth," Grim agreed, following where Rayner's gaze had gone. "Alger and Agee can be trusted. They are the Captains of my Lisa's and my Elite Guards."

"You were found on the Ganglian ship?" Lisa ignored the conversation going on between Grim and Rayner, and moved toward Jennifer.

"No, I was taken by the Ganglians over a year and a half ago."

"A year and a half..." Lisa's eyes widened. "Wait, your name is Jennifer?"

"Yes."

"As in Jennifer Teel?"

"Yes," Jen was surprised this woman made the connection so fast. "Kim is my little sister."

"Oh, my God!" Lisa was immediately hugging Jennifer before any male could move. "Does Kim know? Of course, she knows. What am I saying? She sent you here. She must be ecstatic! But wait..." Lisa pulled back slightly, frowning. "Why are you here? Why aren't you with her and Destiny? She's missed you so much and has been so worried about you."

"And I've missed and been worried about her too." Jen smiled at Lisa. She was just as Kimmy had described her. Beautiful, smart, and caring. "We spent nearly a week together before Warrior Ull arrived." Her expression cooled as she glanced at Ull. "Kimmy wanted me to stay longer, but there are more lives involved here than just ours."

"You're talking about the Ganglian ship full of Earth females the Kaliszians intercepted," Lisa said leading her to one of the couches in the room.

"Yes, Kimmy told me about what happened to you and the other females the Tornians took just like the Ganglians did us."

Grim's displeased growl had both women looking to him, and Rayner moving to step between the King and his True Mate.

"Don't growl at me, King Grim," Jen said glaring at him. "It is no different."

"She's right, Grim," Lisa told him quietly. "I know you did your best, making sure that you only took unprotected females, and that none of us were abused like Kim and Jen were, but that still doesn't make it right."

"I wasn't abused," Jen informed Lisa, "and neither were the women found on the latest Ganglian ship." She ignored Lisa's shocked look and continued. "But the Ganglians aren't as 'selective' as the Tornians. They just swept up any female they found. Young, old, married, single. It didn't matter to them."

"Oh, my God."

"That's why we need to go to Pontus first," Jen glared at Ull. "To get them and return them to Earth, along with the men that were taken with Mac and me."

"Mac?" Lisa asked.

"Mackenzie Wharton. Well, Kozar now," Jen corrected. "She was the female guide that was with us when the Ganglians took us. She's now the True Mate of Treyvon's Second-in-Command, and the other reason we need to get back to Pontus."

"Those females should not be returned," Ull growled.

"That's not your decision," Jen told him, turning angry eyes on him. "They are under the protection of the Kaliszian Empire, and you have been ordered by your Emperor, my sister's husband, to return them safely. And by God, you better or you'd better hope Wray gets to you before I do!"

Grim found his lips twitching as Rayner's True Mate fearlessly challenged the first male of one of the Tornian Empire's most well-thought-of Lords.

"It seems your True Mate is as fearless when dealing with much larger males as my Lisa is," Grim murmured to Rayner.

"She is," Rayner agreed, easing his stance slightly. "She is strong and has survived more than any female should have to. And if you ever growl at her like that again, I will end you. Blood brother to the Emperor or not."

Grim's eyes narrowed for a moment, ignoring the way Alger's and Agee's hands tensed on the hilts of their swords hearing Rayner's threat. "As you should," Grim agreed, and his Captains relaxed. "Just know I feel the same about my Queen."

Looking at each other, the two dominant males realized they had more in common than they ever thought.

∞ ∞ ∞ ∞ ∞

Later that day, Lisa found herself walking the halls of Luanda, absently running a hand over her stomach as she thought over all she had learned that day. Jennifer was truly an amazing woman. They had sat and talked while Grim, Treyvon, and Ull discussed whatever they deemed important, but what she and Jennifer had discussed was so much more.

Not only had the Kaliszians begun to find their True Mates again, some human, some not, they were also able to conceive offspring with humans. It was the other reason Jen wanted to return to Pontus. Her friend, Mackenzie, had conceived with her True Mate and while the two species were similar, the Kaliszians had no real knowledge of how to deal with a pregnant Earth female.

Lisa had immediately understood what Jen wanted. Rebecca to return to Pontus with them. She wanted Rebecca to check Mackenzie and share her knowledge of Earth females with the Kaliszian healer, Luol. Something Lisa knew Grim was going to fight her on. He would want Rebecca to remain on Luda so she could care for her until their daughter was presented. But Lisa knew that wasn't going to be possible. Oh, she wanted Rebecca here when she gave birth. But until then, there were others that needed Rebecca's skills. Jennifer had also confessed that she would like Rebecca to examine *her* because she believed she had also conceived.

Yes, it had been a busy but informative morning, and there was still more that needed to be decided. But first, she needed to check on the girls. Looking up, she saw Nairn approaching.

"You're back from the garden?"

"Yes, Majesty. Cook promised the princesses they could help him make cookies."

"Of course," Lisa smiled. Nothing kept her girls out of the kitchen when Warrior Tagma was making cookies. "Did Miki find her cape?"

"Yes, Majesty."

Lisa had gotten to know the males of Luanda well, especially those of the Elite Guard. She could tell there was something more Nairn wanted to say.

"What is it, Nairn? Did the girls disobey you?"

"No! Of course not, Majesty. The princesses are always well behaved."

"That is an untruth, Nairn," Lisa gently reprimanded. "You know they like to see if they can hide from you."

Nairn smiled slightly. "This is truth, Majesty. So we let them."

"What?!!"

The look on his Queen's face made Nairn realize she had misunderstood, and he quickly reassured her. "We know where they are, Majesty, we just let them *think* we don't."

"Oh, well that's good. Smart, too." Lisa should have realized they would never allow Carly or Miki to get away from them. "So what have they been doing, that they don't think you've noticed, that is bothering you?"

"They are spending a great deal of time beneath one of the trees."

"One of the trees?"

"Yes, it is like the one you had us move into Luanda. The one you called a 'Christmas' tree, except this one has heavy, lower branches that touch the ground."

"So they crawled under it, and you couldn't see them?"

"Yes, Majesty."

"We used to have a tree just like it in our yard back on Earth. They would play underneath it for hours."

"It seems they do here too, but..."

"But what, Nairn?"

"Miki went under it wearing her fur cape. She came back out wearing her purple one."

"She left her fur one there?"

"Yes, and they seemed to be talking, but not to each other."

Lisa frowned at that. "There wasn't anyone else there?"

"No, Majesty."

"There's nothing in the garden that can harm them is there, Nairn? No wild animals?"

"No, Majesty. We would never let them out of our sight if that were the case."

"Of course you wouldn't, Nairn. I know how much you and your brother Warriors care about the girls."

"And you, Majesty," Nairn quickly said, his cheeks darkening slightly.

"Thank you, Nairn," Lisa gave him a small smile. It still surprised her how easily flustered these big, strong Warriors could get when speaking with a female. "I will talk to Grim about this and see what he wants to do. Until you hear from either of us, allow the girls to continue to play under the tree."

"Yes, Majesty."

Chapter Four

"Beneath a tree?" Grim frowned as Lisa told him what she had learned, later that night after the girls were asleep.

"Yes," she said pulling her feet up under her as she cuddled into his side.

Grim reached over and dragged the afghan off the back of the couch, making sure her bare feet were covered, before responding. "There shouldn't be anything in the garden that will harm them, but I will go tomorrow and make sure."

"Thank you," she said gazing up at him.

"You do not need to thank me for seeing to our girls' protection," he told her gruffly.

"I know, but I also know there are a great many other things you need to be seeing to tomorrow. You could just have Ion or Nairn check and report back to you with what they find."

"That is truth, but this is something *I* must see to," Grim reached up touching the glass thumbprints on the necklace he wore. "After all, I am their manno."

"You are," she agreed, smiling up at him sleepily.

"And I am your male." Rising, he scooped her up into his arms. "And now I must see to you."

"Oh you must, must you?" Lisa asked as she pressed a kiss on the thick scar running down his neck.

"Yes," he told her gruffly, "You are tired. You need to rest."

"I am," she agreed, "but I'm never too tired to love my male, and I do, Grim. Love you, that is."

"And I love you, my Lisa."

"Then show me."

"I will," he vowed, and carefully lowering her into their bed, his mouth covered hers.

∞ ∞ ∞ ∞ ∞

A fully rested and fully satisfied Lisa smiled at Grim across the table the next morning as the girls ate. Finally, knowing she needed to pull her thoughts away from what they had done in bed together the night before, she looked to their daughters. "So, girls, there is someone I would like you to meet this morning."

"Who, Mommy?" Carly asked.

"Her name is Jennifer. She is Empress Kim's older sister."

"Older sister? You mean like I am to Miki?"

"Yes, Carly."

"But, Mommy, isn't Kim part of Manno's family?" She looked to Grim. "Part of *our* family?"

"Yes, baby," Lisa told her.

"So then isn't Jennifer part of *our* family too?"

Lisa looked at Grim and realized it was something neither of them had considered, at least not the full extent of it. Yes, Jennifer was now related to them through Kim, but it was more than that. General Rayner was now family too because he was Jennifer's True Mate, and General Rayner was blood-related to Liron, the Emperor of the Kaliszian Empire. The two Empires were now forever connected.

"Yes, Carly, she is. So we need to welcome her into the family."

"But..."

"But what, Miki?" Lisa asked, frowning at her youngest.

"But... we want to go play in the garden."

"Again?" Lisa looked to Grim and saw he was frowning too. While it wasn't uncommon for the girls to play in the garden, they usually didn't play there every day.

"Yes. Pleassse, Mommy." Her amber eyes pleaded with her mother's as she drew out the please, then looked at her manno and did the same thing. "Pleassse, Manno?"

Grim was the most powerful and feared Warrior in the Tornian Empire, but looking into his Miki's eyes, he found himself as defenseless as a first-cycle trainee against an Elite Warrior.

"Why do you wish this so badly, Miki?" Grim questioned quietly.

"Well... uh... because..." Miki stuttered, her panicked gaze going to Carly beseeching her for help.

"We just really like to play out there," Carly said.

"You mean under your tree?" Lisa asked.

"How did you know?" Carly's eyes widened in amazement as she looked back to her mother.

"A little birdie told me," Lisa said teasingly, not wanting the girls to know it had been Nairn that had told her. She didn't want them to think they had no freedom.

"*Prince* told you?" Miki whispered, her little eyes going even wider. "He *talks* to you???"

"Prince?" Lisa asked giving them a confused look. "Who is Prince?"

"The Great Raptor's son," Miki told her as if it were obvious. "He hurt his wing, so we're helping him get better."

"And how are you doing that, Miki?" Grim questioned carefully, finding it took all his Warrior control to keep the alarm out of his voice. Raptors were solitary creatures that rarely attacked without cause. They killed only when it was a matter of survival. They were the symbol of House Luanda because of this. But this Raptor was injured, and even the noblest of creatures could strike out without thought when crazed by pain. The idea of his sweet, innocent daughters being exposed to such a creature made his blood run cold.

"By doing what you do for us, Manno," Miki told him. "We're making sure he's safe, keeping him warm, and bringing him food to eat. And it's working. He seemed better yesterday. Didn't he, Carly?"

"Uh-huh," Carly agreed.

"You found him the day of the Festival?" Lisa looked at her daughters. "That is why you 'forgot' your cape?"

"Prince needed it more, Mommy. He was so cold and scared."

"I don't doubt that, Miki, but you should have come and told your manno or me."

"But we couldn't, Mommy," Miki told her.

"Why, baby?"

"Because... *we* needed to help him. I promised... vowed that we would, and if we don't keep our vows," Miki's little forehead scrunched up as she searched for the word, "then we aren't worthy. Isn't that right, Manno?" She looked to Grim. "It's what you tell your Warriors, isn't it? That 'if you don't keep your vow then you aren't worthy'; and 'you must always protect those that can't protect themselves.' Well, Prince can't defend himself right now, so we have to."

"This is truth," Grim slowly admitted looking from one daughter to the other. He hadn't realized they had been listening that closely to what he told his Warriors. "A vow is a very important thing. But in giving it, you can still ask for help in keeping it, and in this, you should have asked."

"I'm sorry, Manno." Miki's little lips trembled as she looked at him. "I just wanted to be worthy... like you are."

Grim was immediately out of his chair and on his knees between where his two girls sat.

"You are, Miki, you will always be worthy, much worthier than me. You also, Carly."

"Truth, Manno?" Carly asked.

"Truth." He hugged his girls for a moment then rose. "Now, finish your meal, and then we will all go and see your Prince."

"Yes, Manno," they chorused together, and quickly returned to eating.

∞ ∞ ∞ ∞ ∞

It was gray and overcast as the girls led Lisa and Grim to 'their' tree. Grim went down on one knee, then bent even lower still to see under the low bough he had lifted. Behind him, Lisa and the girls waited along with Nairn and Ion. He could understand why the Raptor had chosen this spot. It was well-concealed, and his Warriors wouldn't think a threat could exist in such a compact area. No Tornian male over the age of five would fit inside, but his daughters were much smaller than Tornian youth.

Reaching underneath, Grim pulled out what he found.

"Careful, Manno, Prince doesn't know you." Carly's concern was easily heard. It was something else he was still getting used to. His daughters' unconditional love and concern for him.

"There is nothing here to be concerned with, my Carly," Grim told her as he pulled out the now dirty, but empty, fur cape.

"He's gone," Miki whispered, her amber gaze going from her cape to Grim. "He didn't even say goodbye."

Suddenly, a loud screech filled the air above them, and every head looked up and found the Raptor sitting on one of the uppermost branches of the tree, staring down at them.

"My God," Lisa murmured quietly, taking in the size of the bird. She had pictured a much smaller creature in her mind, not one that seemed nearly as tall has her youngest. Its body was just as black and sleek looking as the one Gahan had created that now sat in Grim's Command Room. And while his wings rested against his body, there was no doubting he was as deadly as any Elite Warrior with his sharp, curved beak and long, lethal claws. Yet she could see the intelligence in the piercing purple of his eyes. No wonder he was the symbol for House Luanda.

Just the thought of her innocent daughters being near such a creature, let alone feeding it, sent a shiver of apprehension up Lisa's spine.

"Prince." Miki's little hands rested on her hips as she looked up and found him. There wasn't an ounce of fear in her voice. "What are you doing up there? You are supposed to be resting. We brought you first meal." Reaching into her pocket, she pulled out the piece of rashtar she'd saved from their first meal and held it up to him.

With a swiftness no one would expect from such a large, presumably injured creature, the Raptor swooped down to land directly in front of Miki.

Lisa gasped.

Ion and Nairn moved forward.

Grim drew his sword.

But the Raptor's intense, violet gaze remained fixed on Miki.

"Oh, you're better," she exclaimed happily, unaware of the tension that filled the adults around her, and apparently unconcerned that a deadly bird nearly as tall as she was had just landed in front of her. "I'm so glad. Here." She held out the rashtar to him.

Lisa held her breath as the Raptor's sharp, deadly beak lowered toward the soft, unprotected skin of her youngest's fingers. But it only bit at the rashtar, seeming to know it could harm Miki if he weren't careful.

"Prince, this is my mommy and my manno," Miki told the bird. She had watched her mommy and knew it was rude not to introduce people. "Mommy, Manno, this is Prince."

"I..." Lisa looked to Grim for a moment. She had never been introduced to a bird before, but this seemed to be important to her daughter, so she went along. "Hello, Prince," she said and bowed slightly to the bird just as she would for a real Prince. She was shocked when he returned the gesture, bowing deeper than she had, as a Prince would to a Queen. It then turned its intense gaze to Grim.

Grim was completely shocked by what was happening. While his bedtime stories about the Great Raptor had been filled with how the creature acted and responded just as an Elite Warrior would, they had been just stories handed down so a young male would know what was expected of him. No one actually thought them to be true, at least not once they grew older. But here his girls were, treating and talking to one, exactly as he had told them they should. And the Raptor was responding.

"Prince." Grim lowered his sword but didn't sheath it as he bowed his head to the creature.

The Raptor eyed the sword for a moment before it again seemed to bow to the King of Luda.

Suddenly, a deafening clap of thunder rolled across the land, and a curtain of rain began advancing toward them. With a great screech, Prince spread his wings and launched himself into the sky.

"Inside, now!" Sheathing his sword, Grim scooped Miki and Carly up, one in each arm. Then using his massive frame, he protected Lisa from the wind as he moved them toward Luanda. When tempests like this suddenly appeared, they were deadly.

Ion and Nairn held open the doors as Grim rushed his family inside, closing them just as a blinding flash of light lit up the garden. It had both girls screaming out in fright.

"Calm, little ones. You are safe."

"But Prince, Manno." Miki looked up at him, tears filling her eyes.

"He is safe," Grim reassured her. "This is what he does."

"Your vow?" she asked, her bottom lip trembling.

"My vow, my Miki."

∞ ∞ ∞ ∞ ∞

Lisa found she was still somewhat shaken by what happened in the garden, and the rumble of the continuing storm wasn't helping to calm her nerves.

For her girls to have been so close to such a dangerous creature.

For her and Grim to not even be aware it was there.

For the tempest to appear so suddenly.

She had to fight against holding the little hands of her girls too tightly as they walked toward Grim's Command Room. She thought she'd been aware of all the dangers their new home contained, but every day she found herself learning something new. Like how a dangerous bird could be in their garden. Grim had understood that she needed to make sure her babies were okay and had gone ahead to meet the shuttle containing Ull, General Rayner, and Jennifer. Entering Grim's Command Room, she saw that everyone was there.

"I'm sorry we kept you waiting."

"It is fine, my Lisa," Grim reassured her, moving from behind his desk.

"Girls, this is Warrior Ull of House Rigel," Lisa began the introductions.

"I remember you," Carly piped in looking up at Ull. "You were at the Joining Ceremony."

Ull frowned as the taller of the young females spoke to him without permission.

"My daughter is speaking to you, Warrior Ull." Grim's deep growl expressed his displeasure at Ull's lack of response to Carly.

"I was," Ull stiltedly responded. He would never get used to these Earth females talking whenever they wished.

"You are Ynyr's brother," Carly continued, unfazed by the lack of warmth on Ull's face or in his tone.

"Yes, his older brother."

"Really? But he's already a Lord," she said giving him a confused look.

"And this is General Treyvon Rayner of the Kaliszian Empire," Lisa quickly went on, pulling Carly's gaze away from Ull. She knew from her conversations with Abby that Ull was still having trouble dealing with the fact that his *younger* brother had become a Lord before him. That, and that Abby chose Ynyr over him.

"Wow," Miki whispered, and letting go of her mother's hand, moved across the room coming to a stop in front of Treyvon. "You're almost as handsome as our manno."

"He is not!" Carly immediately defended Grim. "Manno is handsomer."

"I said *almost*," Miki spun around to argue with her sister. "Because Manno will always be much handsomer than any male in the Known Universes."

"It's more handsome," Lisa quietly corrected her daughters, while trying to keep the smile off her face. Especially when she saw the range of expressions crossing the males' faces.

Ull's was blank in shock. Treyvon's was obviously trying to hold back his amusement. But Grim's was the most expressive of all, at least to her. An unhappy frown had crossed his face at the thought that another male might rival him in Miki's eyes, but his chest had expanded with unadulterated pride at how both his daughters thought and spoke of him.

"That's enough, girls," Lisa said gently but firmly, knowing their argument would grow if she didn't stop it. "You both need to tell General Rayner you're sorry."

"Unnecessary," Treyvon began, but Lisa's piercing look silenced him.

"Yes, it is, General Rayner. Sometimes our girls forget their manners." Her gaze returned to her daughters. "Don't you, girls?"

"Yes, Mommy," they chorused together then turned to Treyvon. "Sorry."

Treyvon found himself trapped for a moment by their amber gazes before giving them a slight bow, letting them know he accepted their apology.

"And this," Lisa gestured to Jennifer, who had remained silent next to Treyvon, "is Jennifer, General Rayner's True Mate."

"Oh, you're Kim's sister!" Miki clapped her hands excitedly as she looked to Jennifer.

"I am," Jennifer agreed.

"Welcome to the family!"

"What?" Jennifer gave Lisa a confused look.

"Carly pointed out at first meal this morning that we are now family since your sister is married to Grim's brother." Lisa looked to Treyvon. "Which means you are now family too, General. Our families and Empires are now forever linked."

A sharp bolt of lightning, instantly followed by a window-rattling crack of thunder, prevented anyone from responding.

Chapter Five

"Manno!" the girls screamed as the room went dark for a moment after the brilliant flash of light. Grim was immediately there, wrapping them up in his protective arms.

"Calm, little ones," he murmured. "We are inside. Remember? You are safe."

"But Prince..." Miki looked up at him with wide, fear-filled eyes.

"Is with *his* manno, who is protecting him just like I am protecting you."

"You're sure?" she questioned, her little chin trembling.

"I'm sure, Miki."

"Hey, how would you like Ion and Nairn to take you to Cook?" Lisa asked as she gently rubbed each of the girls' backs. "I happen to know that he is planning on making more cookies today."

"Truth?" Carly asked, her eyes hopeful.

"Truth."

The girls looked at each other for a moment, then wiggled in Grim's arms to be released. And after each kissing one of his cheeks, they were gone.

∞ ∞ ∞ ∞ ∞

"What kind?" The chef in Jennifer had to ask, and she found herself pinned by the powerful gazes of both the King and Queen of Luda.

It was Lisa who finally answered. "The Tornian version of shortbread cookies."

"Really? I'd love to get the recipe."

"I forgot, you were a Chef back on Earth."

"She is a Chef here also," Treyvon growled. "Her skills have enhanced the lives of our people. Her cookies and brownies are highly prized."

Lisa put a gentle hand on Grim's arm, knowing he wasn't going to like the way the General was talking to her.

41

"Of course she is, General," Lisa pacified and gestured to the sitting area, something that had been added to Grim's Command Room since her arrival. "I meant no offense. As I said, I had just forgotten."

As they all sat, Lisa frowned at Jennifer. "Brownies?"

"Yes." Jennifer's hand mimicked Lisa's, soothing her own mate. "One of the Zaludian ships Treyvon intercepted was carrying chocolate from Earth."

"Honestly?" Lisa's eyes widened in excitement, and for a moment she reminded Treyvon of her daughters.

"Yes, they seemed to have cleared out an entire baking aisle."

"So you have *chocolate*?"

Grim frowned at the way his Lisa stressed the unknown word. Her tone was filled with such awe and desire that he'd only ever heard before when she was in his arms.

"Yes. We have chocolate chips, chocolate chunks, chocolate bars, milk chocolate, bitter chocolate, dark chocolate, even white chocolate, and cocoa powder."

"What is this... chocolate?" Grim demanded. If it were something his Lisa desired so greatly, he would make sure she had it.

"It's something incredible from Earth," Lisa told him, her eyes still fixed on Jennifer.

"That is truth," Treyvon agreed. "My Warriors never miss last meal when my Jennifer prepares something with it. Empress Kim has even threatened your brother that she will give him no more offspring unless he has a supply of it on hand."

"What?!!" It was Grim's eyes that widened this time.

"Totally understandable," Lisa nodded, rubbing her baby bump then demanded. "What will it cost me to get some?"

∞ ∞ ∞ ∞ ∞

"Cook?" Carly looked up from the bowl she was stirring to the old Warrior who was helping her sister.

"What is it, little one?" Tagma asked, smiling down at Miki, letting her know she was doing a fine job even though he'd have to throw that mixture out, before turning his attention to Carly.

He couldn't believe how life had changed in House Luanda since the arrival of these precious little females and their mother. He'd been a bitter, old Warrior who the Goddess hadn't seen fit to bless with a female or with the glory of dying in battle. Instead, as his skills had waned with age, he'd had to return to the kitchens and use the skills his manno had taught him before he'd begun his Warrior training.

For years now he'd begrudged his position, seeing it as a stigma of his failings instead of a chance for a different, better life. And his life was better, thanks to these little ones. They looked at what he did with such awe and wonder that it filled him with pride that being a Warrior never had. They wanted to learn from him, and it made him see his position differently, made him a different male.

"What do you know about the Great Raptor?" she asked, setting her bowl aside.

"The Great Raptor?" he asked frowning slightly.

"Uh-huh."

"Doesn't Ki..." he broke off. He knew the little ones now called King Grim, manno. The news of this had spread faster than a solar storm through the Festival. It was yet another sign of how worthy these females found Grim. "Doesn't your manno tell you about him?"

"Oh, yes. Manno tells us a new story every night."

"Really good stories," Miki added, not wanting to be left out of the conversation.

"Then why do you want *me* to tell you one?"

Carly just shrugged her little shoulders. "I just thought that maybe your manno told you different stories."

"My manno did tell me tales of the Great Raptor."

"Really?" Setting her bowl aside now, Miki plopped her elbows on the counter, her chin propped up on top of her hands, just like her sister had. "Did he tell you any about Prince?"

"Prince?" he gave her a confused look.

"Yeah, the Great Raptor's son," Carly replied as if it should be obvious.

"We met him in the garden," Miki told him. "He was hurt, and we helped him."

"What!?!" Tagma roared, startling the girls. The reflexes he thought had waned with age were never faster as he steadied them both on their stools. It also had Ion and Nairn rushing into the kitchen, swords drawn, until Tagma shook his head at them telling them that everything was fine.

"I am sorry, little ones," he continued, his voice lowering as he dropped to his knees. "I did not mean to frighten you."

"Wh... why were you upset?" Miki asked, her little voice trembling.

"I was just surprised. That is all." Tagma's mind was racing to find a way to explain his terror at the thought of these precious, little ones being so close to such a dangerous creature. "It is a very rare thing to see the Great Raptor, let alone his... son."

"Really?" Carly asked.

"Yes. My manno told me that it is a great honor for one to see... Prince."

"Really?"

"Yes. You see while the Great Raptor is out protecting the people of Luda, Prince stays behind protecting the Great Raptor's mate, his mother. Although it is said that *she* is as deadly as her mate, especially when it comes to defending those she loves."

"Like mommy is."

"Yes, little one, just like your mommy."

"They must have been so worried. Prince was in the garden for two days. Manno and Mommy would be if it were us."

"They would be," Tagma said, his throat tightening at the thought and as his gaze rose to Ion's and Nairn's. They all knew that the King and Queen of Luda wouldn't be just *worried* if their little ones were missing for two days. They would be heartsick and *enraged*! Grim would tear all of Luda apart to find them.

"So others have met Prince?" Carly asked.

"I only know of one other." Tagma thought of a story his manno had only told him once. "My manno told me that there was once a Warrior who did as the two of you have done."

"Really?"

"Yes. He found, protected, and healed an injured Raptor. Because of this, the Raptor gifted the Warrior a piece of himself."

"What did he give him?" Miki whispered.

"The Eye of the Raptor. Here." Tagma held open his hand and pointed to an unmarked spot in his palm between his thumb and forefinger where two lines met and faintly resembled a bird's head. "It allowed the Warrior to sense evil, and have the power to destroy it, protecting those under his care. As the Great Raptor does."

"Wow..." the girls both whispered, then looked at their own palms that were as unmarked as Tagma's, and were disappointed.

"Do not worry, little ones. The Eye of the Raptor has only been gifted once in all of known time, but you were still honored by meeting Prince. It has been hundreds of years since *anyone* has been given that honor. Don't you agree, Ion?" Tagma looked to the younger Warrior for help.

"Many hundreds," Ion agreed. "So long ago that I cannot even recall the last Warrior's name."

"Wow, so we are the first females to meet him?" Carly asked, her eyes going wide.

"Yes."

"That's so cool," the girls whispered looking at each other.

∞ ∞ ∞ ∞ ∞

"You believe this 'recording' will be enough?" Ull skeptically asked after Lisa had finished speaking.

"It will be a start, at least for Trisha. I have no doubt she's been trying to figure out what happened to the girls and me. The problem is going to be you getting close enough to her to get her to listen to it, especially after the way the Ganglians took the last group of women."

"That won't be a problem."

"You think you'll be able to just 'get close' to the niece of the President of the United States? A female he considers his daughter? It would be like Grim allowing an unknown male close to any of our girls."

That had Ull snapping his mouth shut because he knew how carefully King Grim guarded his females. That *he* was even allowed to see them had surprised him.

"So you are going to have to approach when she is alone and convince her to view the recording before her guards attack. And no!" Lisa gave him a sharp look. "You can't just kill them. You are trying to build a relationship between the Tornian Empire and Earth. Your first act there can't be killing people."

Ull growled his displeasure at that.

"You also can't force the educator on her," Lisa told him in a hard voice and could see that had been his plan. "I won't subject Trisha to what the rest of us have had to go through. Trisha will either do this or not."

"And if it's not?" Ull growled.

"Then we'll have to find another way. I know I can get you enough time for Trisha to at least consider using the educator, but you and your actions will be the deciding factor." Lisa turned concerned eyes to Grim who sat beside her on the couch. "Are you and Wray sure Warrior Ull is the best male for this? Maybe I..."

Ull's roar of outrage drowned out the rest of what she was going to say as Ull surged out of his chair. Grim was instantly on his feet and in front of his Lisa, his sword drawn and pointing at Ull. General Rayner did the same, standing protectively in front of his Jennifer, but ready to assist the King if needed.

"You will not threaten *my Queen*, Warrior Ull. First male or not, I will end you if you take so much as a step toward her."

"She *dares* to question my worthiness in this!"

"When you act like this, then yes, I do." Lisa rose, and while she moved to where she could see Ull, she remained behind Grim. "This is too important, and not just for the Tornians, but also the Kaliszians and the people of Earth. Females are not possessions on Earth, Warrior Ull. They aren't going to just obey you because you are male. We are independent creatures. We make our own decisions, choose how we want to live our lives, and speak our minds. You've shown time and time again that you have trouble accepting that. Something I find difficult to believe with a mother like Isis."

"My mother..."

"Is a remarkable female." Lisa cut him off. "She stood up for what she believed in, for what she wanted, and for who she loved. That you can't appreciate that is what makes me question that you are the right male for this task. Trisha has had to survive and deal with a great deal. She's strong and independent. She isn't going to put up with your bullshit attitude toward females. She's dealt with enough assholes in her life."

"Assholes?" Ull questioned.

"Unworthy and unfit males," Lisa clarified for him. "Ones that only want to use her for their own gains."

"I am not an asshole," Ull grumbled as he sat back down.

"Maybe not to other males, but to Earth females... Jennifer?" Lisa looked to Rayner's True Mate.

"Total asshole," Jennifer agreed.

"Look, Ull," Lisa's voice softened as she moved to sit back down, and slowly Grim followed. "I know what happened at the Joining Ceremony still bothers you. That you see not being selected as a reflection of your worth, but it wasn't. It had absolutely nothing to do with *you*. You could have been the worthiest male the Known Universes have ever seen, and *still,* you wouldn't have been chosen."

"Ynyr was," the words slipped passed his lips before he could stop them.

"Truth," Lisa gave him a sympathetic look.

∞ ∞ ∞ ∞ ∞

"Maybe I should be the one going to Earth," Lisa whispered later that night as she lay in Grim's arms, a hand absently caressing his chest as she gazed out the windows at the star-filled sky.

"No."

"But, Grim..."

"You are with offspring, Lisa."

"Truth, but that doesn't mean..."

"I would not let you go without me."

"I wouldn't want to."

"What of the girls? The other females? Do we leave them behind? Who will help and protect them if we do?"

Lisa's heart clenched at the thought of being so far away from her babies if they happened to need her. She knew someday that time would come, but that wasn't today. Then there were the other Earth females. The invited males had begun arriving, and she needed to be here to help supervise the meetings and calm fears. Releasing a deep sigh, she looked up at him. "You're right. My place, *our* place is here on Luda, but Ull is still so angry, and I don't understand why."

"He is the first male of a Lord, my Lisa. He was brought up to believe *he* would be the first, and most likely only male, in his bloodline to obtain a female."

"But why? He has three younger brothers."

"Which is unheard of. You know this, my Lisa. A female might stay with the same male long enough to give him two males, but *four*? It cast a stigma on House Rigel. No Kaliszian female would consider joining with anyone other than the future Lord."

"And then Abby chose Ynyr, a third male."

"Yes."

"But if he wants a female so badly, why didn't he put in his application to meet any of the women?"

"Pride. His younger brother is now the most powerful Lord in the Empire. He has a female, and she is already with offspring."

"Well, he'd better get over it before he gets to Earth."

"He is a Warrior. He will put his feelings aside and do what is required of him."

"He'd better," Lisa said, then forgetting Ull, stretched up so her bare breasts barely brushed his chest as she teased. "Now there is something I require of the Warrior beneath me."

"What does my Queen require of me?" Grim asked, his shaft hardening as she shifted over him, her already slick channel brushing it.

"For you to love me, my King."

"I do," Grim growled as he slowly entered her and began to thrust. "I always will. For you are my Queen. My Lisa. My everything."

With every declaration, Grim thrust harder, deeper, and the passion that never took much to rekindle between them ignited into a solar storm.

"Goddess yes, Grim!" Lisa cried out as she pressed her hands against his chest and arching her back, began to ride him. "You are mine. My King. My Grim. My everything."

"Then give me everything that is mine, my Lisa," he ordered, knowing neither of them was going to last long. Not with the way she was already tightening around him. Capturing one of the lush breasts she was so readily offering, he sucked it deep into his mouth the way he knew always pushed her over the edge, especially now that she carried his offspring.

"Grim!" she screamed as her release hit.

"Lisa!" Grim roared as he followed, and together they experienced heaven.

Chapter Six

"Jen, I would like you to meet Rebecca Mines." Lisa introduced the two females the next morning in the sun room, after she had her guards exit, closing the door behind them. "Dr. Rebecca Mines, OB/GYN. Rebecca, this is Jennifer Rayner, General Rayner's True Mate, and Kim's sister."

"Sister?" Rebecca's eyes widened. "The one Kim was looking for when the Ganglians captured her?"

"Yes," Jen answered. "They'd taken me, and the group I was with, six months earlier."

"Wow. What are the chances of that?"

'Probably better than you think,' Jen thought but said nothing.

"Come, let's sit," Lisa gestured to the conversation area that sat in front of the wall of windows that let sunshine stream into the room.

"Wow, that's really beautiful," Jen said moving to get a closer look at the suncatcher that hung in the window. It was a myriad of colors that made you think it was just haphazardly put together, but on closer inspection, she could see the pattern repeated, like in a kaleidoscope. The shards of color it gave off in the morning light were amazing.

"Isn't it?" Lisa agreed smiling. "Dagan made it for me for the Festival of the Goddess."

"Dagan?"

"He's our clothiers, Padma's and Gossamer's, second male. He's very special."

"I'd say." Finally taking a chair, Jen waited, and Lisa turned her gaze to Rebecca.

"Rebecca, the reason I wanted you to meet us here is that there is something I need to talk to you about. And it can't go any further than this room."

"Alright..." Rebecca's gaze traveled from Lisa to Jen and back again.

"More women have been taken from Earth," Lisa told her bluntly.

"What?!!" She shot up stiffly in her chair. "Wray sent..."

"No!" Lisa cut her off. "Wray vowed to Kim that he wouldn't, and he hasn't."

"Then who?" Rebecca shot accusing eyes to Jen. "The Kaliszians?"

"Wrong again," Jen told her, her gaze hard. "The Kaliszians saved them. It was the Ganglians."

"The Ganglians..." Rebecca's words trailed off. "Oh, my God. How many survived?"

"All of them," Jen informed her. "The Ganglians didn't take them to rape. They kidnapped them so they could sell them to Tornian warriors on Vesta."

"What? No!" Rebecca denied, looking physically ill. "Callen would never..."

"Of course he wouldn't," Lisa quickly reassured her. "This was done by Reeve."

"Callen discovered this?" Rebecca asked, the color slowly returning to her face.

"No, the Kaliszians did when they intercepted a Ganglian ship in their Empire."

"I don't understand."

"Look, the Kaliszians have been intercepting Ganglian and Zaludian ships ever since Wray was shot down over Pontus," Jen told her. "They've been trying to figure out why the two are working together and they think they might have figured it out."

"And that is?"

"To disrupt the balance of power by supplying Tornian males with compatible females, and the Kaliszian people with food. If they do this, then *they* will become the two most powerful species in the Known Universes."

"But there's no way they can do that," Rebecca argued. "Neither species has a home world."

"They could because they know where Earth is, and they are the only ones, as Wray has kept its location a secret."

"But you said the Kaliszians have been intercepting their ships."

"And every time we do, they've been able to delete their navigational data. It's one of the reasons Treyvon and I wanted to speak to Wray. We want to return the women to Earth, but can't because we don't know where it is."

"And if it becomes known that there are compatible Earth females in the Kaliszian Empire..." Lisa trailed off.

"It could mean war," Rebecca whispered.

"Yes. Some of the Warriors are getting desperate, Rebecca. If they attack..."

"Treyvon and Liron would defend them. They would have no choice, not after what Aadi did."

"Alright. So what's the plan and why are you telling *me* this? I'm just a doctor."

"The plan is for Ull to go to Earth and make contact, explain what is happening, and try to negotiate a treaty that will not only protect Earth but help the Tornians and Kaliszians."

"The Tornians kidnapping us isn't going to help with that."

"We know, which is why Ull is following Jen and General Rayner to Pontus first, to pick up the women they rescued and return them to Earth."

"Along with the surviving men from the group I was taken with," Jen added.

"But not us."

"No, Rebecca, I'm sorry. I tried to get Wray to let you be returned too, but..."

"He refused."

"My new brother-in-law can be a real asshole," Jen muttered, "but in this, I have to agree with him."

"Of course you would!" Rebecca accused. "You've had it pretty cushy, haven't you? True Mate to a General. Sister to the Empress."

"Rebecca," Lisa tried to cut her off.

"Cushy?!!" Jen growled. "I've had it *cushy*? What do you know about it? Were you captured by the Ganglians? Were you forced to witness them *raping* females? Were you sold as a slave? Made to work in a mine? To live in a cave! Were you starved, Rebecca? Was your husband beaten to death right before your eyes? Did you cry every night and wish you could just *die*?"

"I…" Rebecca was cut off by the doors of the sunroom being slammed open, and a male she had never seen storming through them, despite the guards trying to stop him. He was instantly in front of Jennifer, pulling her up and into his arms.

"What is wrong, my Jennifer? Who has upset you?"

Grim stormed in bare seconds after Treyvon, his sword pulled. "Lisa?"

"It's all right, Grim. Things just got a little… heated."

"It's my fault." Rebecca slowly stood, her eyes full of regret and just a little fear of the large, Kaliszian General. His hard, glowing gaze pinned her even while he still gently held Jen. "I didn't understand her situation. I just assumed she'd been safe in the Kaliszian Empire all this time."

"While it is truth she has been in our Empire since her abduction, she has been far from safe," Treyvon growled.

"I gathered that. I'm sorry, Jen. Truly," she said when Jen looked at her over a massive bicep. "I usually don't just jump to conclusions like that, but lately…"

"Your life's been in turmoil."

"Yes."

"It's okay, Treyvon," she reached up to gently caress his cheek. "You can put me down. I overreacted too, and I have a feeling that's going to be happening a lot more for a while."

"What do you mean?" Treyvon asked, slowly putting her back on her feet. And while he released her, one hand stayed on the small of her back.

"I'll get to that, but first." She turned to face Rebecca. "I'm sorry too, Rebecca. I should have explained myself better when I said I agreed with

Wray. I didn't mean that you should have to stay here, have to Join with a Tornian. What I meant was, for right now, we need to proceed as if nothing has changed. If the Ganglians or Zaludians find out what we were trying to do..."

"Lisa! You told her?" Grim frowned down at his Queen.

"She has the right to know if she's going to help," Lisa told him, not intimidated in the least at his fierce frown.

"Out!" Grim turned to face the guards. "Close the doors. No one enters."

"Yes, sire!"

"They were supposed to be doing that before," Lisa's lips twitched looking at Treyvon.

"No one keeps a Kaliszian away from his True Mate," Treyvon told her. "Especially when he knows she is in distress."

"How did you know?" Rebecca asked looking confused. "Were you walking right by? We weren't *that* loud were we?"

"It's a True Mate thing," Jen told her, not willing to go any further than that. "So are we okay? With what I said I mean? I would understand why you wouldn't be, what with not being allowed to go back too."

"Yes," Rebecca said nodding.

"Thank you, because the reason we're telling you this is that we need to ask for your help."

"*My* help?"

"Yes, as a doctor. You see there was another female with us when we were taken. Mackenzie, Mac."

"And she's not returning to Earth with the other females?"

"No, she's the True Mate to Treyvon's Second-in-Command, Nikhil... and she's pregnant."

"I see."

"It was the other reason Treyvon and I wanted to meet with Wray and get him to tell us Earth's location. We were going to go there to find my sister and bring back the information Luol, our Healer, would need to make sure Mac had a safe pregnancy. We didn't know that the new Empress was my little sister. Or that you were here."

"It must have been a shocking reunion."

"It was, especially meeting little Destiny." A smile filtered across her lips as she thought of Destiny. "Thank you by the way." Her gaze included Lisa. "Kimmy told me she couldn't have done it without the two of you."

"Kim and Rebecca did all the hard work. I was just there for support," Lisa said, downplaying her part.

"You were there for more than that. Kimmy told me how you, Rebecca, took a knife in the back to protect Destiny and that you, Lisa, distracted that psycho Risa long enough for Kim to get her out of the room."

Neither woman said anything.

"Which is why I'm hoping you'll come to Pontus with us and help Mac."

"Is this Nikhil as big as him?" Rebecca motioned to Treyvon.

"Bigger."

"Bigger?" Lisa and Rebecca said in disbelief.

"Commander Nikhil is one of the largest and most powerful Kaliszians in our Empire," Treyvon told them quietly. "He is also deeply concerned that because of this, the offspring the Goddess has blessed them with might harm his True Mate. If you were able to assist our Healer in making sure that doesn't happen, the Kaliszian Empire would be in your debt."

"As will I," Treyvon said giving Jennifer a hard look. "For I believe my True Mate is with offspring but has yet to tell me."

"I wanted Rebecca to check me first to be sure. You saw how Nikhil lost control when he just thought Mac might be."

"One of your Elite Warriors lost control?" Grim questioned moving slightly closer to Lisa.

"But for a moment. Earth females are smaller than ours. Are you saying you haven't feared for your Queen?" Treyvon looked at the difference in size between Grim and Lisa.

"I have," Grim acknowledged quietly, and the two males shared an understanding look. "Which is why if you choose to go with them, Rebecca, I must demand you be here for the presentation of our daughter." He put a protective arm around Lisa, pulling her close.

"Of course I would be," Rebecca quickly reassured Grim. "But Hadar now has enough knowledge to care for Lisa if I'm gone for a while. He did just fine when I went to check Abby."

"This is truth, Grim," Lisa looked up at him reassuringly. "And I can make sure Rebecca does a thorough scan before she leaves if that helps."

"She will," Grim growled.

"I will," Rebecca agreed.

∞ ∞ ∞ ∞ ∞

"I really don't see why this is necessary," Rebecca said for the third time as she looked at Lisa. "The coverings I have will be fine."

"Jen said it's warm on Pontus right now, like summer back on Earth. Not winterish like it is here right now. Because of that, Padma and Caitir have been concentrating on making warmer coverings, but you're going to need something else."

"I wish the General would have let Jen come with us."

"I doubt Treyvon is going to let Jen out of his sight for a while. Not after you confirmed she's with offspring."

"Yeah, I still don't know if his reaction was cute or just damn scary."

"You mean wrapping her up in his arms, growling at everyone, and immediately carrying her back to their rooms?" Lisa asked chuckling. "Grim would have done the same to me if we hadn't been in the middle of the Assembly when he found out."

"That's true." Rebecca smiled remembering the King of Luda's reaction to Lisa announcing she carried his offspring.

"And besides, the girls wanted to see Dagan. Didn't you, girls?" She looked at Carly and Miki who were sitting across from them.

"Uh-huh," they replied. "It's been *forever* since we've gotten to play with him."

"It's only been a week," Lisa reminded them.

"Like we said," Miki told them. "*Forever.*"

"I'm also surprised Grim let *you* come alone." Rebecca gave her a questioning look. Everyone knew how protective the King of Luda was of his family, especially with warriors arriving.

"I'd hardly say I was *alone*," Lisa gave Rebecca an exasperated look. "There are three transports full of guards with us."

"Like I said, alone," Rebecca teased. Their transport coming to a stop ended the conversation.

"Come on, Mommy, let's go," Miki said reaching for the handle.

"Miki Renee, you know better," Lisa gently admonished her youngest. "We have to wait until Agee or Kirk open the door." It was a small concession for her to give if it helped Grim to not worry so much.

"Oh, yeah. I forgot. Sorry, Mommy."

"It's alright, baby. I know you were just excited, but you need to try to remember so your manno doesn't worry."

"Yes, Mommy."

Looking up as the door opened, Lisa saw Agee standing there holding out a hand.

"My Queen, the area is secure."

Taking his hand, Lisa let him help her out of the transport. It was something that was getting more and more difficult the further along she got in pregnancy.

"Thank you, Agee," she said giving him an apologetic smile, knowing he was going to have to be doing this more and more as she got heavier.

"It is not a problem, my Queen," Agee told her quietly. Then making sure Kirk was there, turned to assist Rebecca and the girls.

"Lisa," Padma called out as she walked down the path toward the transports. "What are you doing here? Why didn't you call? I would have come to you."

"I know you would have," Lisa laughed, hugging her first true friend on Luda, "but the girls wanted to play with Dagan, and honestly I wanted to get out for a while."

"Is everything okay?" Padma asked running a critical eye over her friend and Queen, as well as the number of guards that were surrounding them.

"Of course it is. Grim would never have let me out of his sight if it wasn't."

"That is truth," Padma agreed smiling slightly as she gestured toward her open door. "Come inside and we'll talk, or would you rather sit out back? It isn't that cold out today. Not with the way the sun is beating down."

"Actually, I need to speak with you about making some cooler coverings."

"For you?" Padma frowned as they waited for the guards to say her home was secure. Once that was done, they entered her home.

"No, for Rebecca," Lisa told her once the door was closed.

"I see," Padma said but didn't. "Girls, Dagan is out back."

"Can we go find him, Mommy?" Carly asked.

"Yes. Take either Agee or Kirk with you."

"Yes, Mommy," they chorused as they rushed out the back door.

Chapter Seven

"Look, it's the idiot."

Dagan looked up to find three young males moving toward him. He didn't like them. They were new to Luda, having recently been sent here by their mannos so the Empire's Greatest Warrior, King Grim, could train them. But when they weren't training, they liked to sneak out of House Luanda and terrorize the countryside. One day, they had discovered Dagan walking along the creek picking up pretty stones. At first, he thought they had wanted to play with him, the way Carly and Miki did, but he quickly discovered what they considered *fun* was to shove him to the ground and hit him.

The last time they'd found him, he'd gone home with his shirt torn and his body bruised. He'd lied to his mama and said he'd fallen, not only because he sometimes did, but because he knew she would be upset if he told her truth.

No one had hit him since Gahan had left the King's Glassmaker's shop, and his mama had been so happy since then. Dagan didn't want her to be sad again.

"Go away," Dagan said, backing away from them.

"Oh look, it talks," Eero, the smallest of the three, sneered. He was the one that seemed to enjoy hurting Dagan the most.

"I didn't think he could do anything but cry," Lalo, the biggest one, said.

"Let's see how long it will take this time." Dal, the leader of the three, leaned down picking up a thick stick as the other two moved to surround Dagan.

Dagan's gaze widened as he turned in a tight circle searching for a way out.

"Oh no, you unfit spawn, there's no way out this time." Dal raised the stick. "Your manno should have ended you before you drew your first breath. But since he wasn't male enough to do it, *we* will." With that, he started swinging, and with a cry, Dagan dropped to the ground protecting his head.

∞ ∞ ∞ ∞ ∞

"Come on, Miki," Carly called out over her shoulder as she ran up the path. "I think I hear Dagan in the meadow."

The path in the woods was one the girls had been down before. It led to the small furnace that Gossamer had built for his first male, Gahan, so that he could practice his glass making skills. Dagan had shown it to them on one of their visits, confiding that he liked to go there.

Bursting into the meadow, Carly came to an abrupt halt when she saw three young males circling Dagan. She hadn't known Dagan had play dates with other friends, especially ones so close to his age.

"What game are they playing?" Miki asked, coming to stand beside her sister.

"I don't know."

"I don't like them," Miki said frowning. "They look mean."

"You know what Mommy says about judging people by how they look."

"I know but..." Just then, Dagan fell to the ground, and the three started hitting and kicking him.

"Stop that!" Carly yelled and began running directly toward the boys. When she got closer, she launched herself at the one swinging the stick. She aimed for his knees the way she'd seen one of the Warriors do at the Festival. During that match, the Warriors hadn't even been allowed stingers, and the smaller one had won the match with just such a move. Her manno had grunted his approval.

Dal didn't know what was happening. One minute he was standing there beating the idiot, the next he was on the ground, the stick flying from his grip. Kicking out, he found his attacker was gone, having rolled away with a skill *he* still hadn't mastered. Looking up, he found himself staring up into the furious amber eyes of... a *female*?

"You *will not* hurt Dagan like that!" she growled at him.

"You are bad males," Miki hissed, dropping to her knees beside Dagan. "Evil."

The other two had stopped attacking when Dal had.

"What the..." Lalo looked from the young female that had suddenly appeared next to Dagan, to the other one who was now holding the stick over Dal like it was a sword.

"You will leave. Now!" Carly ordered.

Dal's light, green-skinned face flushed emerald with embarrassment and anger that this... female would think to tell him what to do. Jumping to his feet, he took a threatening step toward her. "You *dare* speak to a warrior like that?"

"You're not a warrior," Carly told him not backing down. "Warriors are fit and worthy. They protect those smaller and weaker than them. They *don't* attack them. When I tell my manno what you've done, he's going to be angry."

"Yeah," Miki nodded in agreement, "*really* angry."

"Not if you can't tell him," Dal growled as he ripped the branch from Carly's hands and raised it. "Get her, too," he ordered the other two, gesturing with his head toward Miki.

Dagan reared up, wrapping his larger body around Miki, so he took the kicks aimed at her, and cried out "No!" But it was drowned out by an enraged screech that rent the air.

∞ ∞ ∞ ∞ ∞

Lisa looked up, surprised when she saw Grim striding into Padma's cottage.

"Grim, what are you doing here?" she asked as she rose, moving toward him with a smile on her lips.

"I felt the need to be with you," he told her quietly as he leaned down kissing her lips gently.

"We haven't been gone that long. Not even an hour."

"Yet you were gone," he said as if that was enough of an explanation. "Where are the girls?" he asked looking around the room, his gaze taking in their absence.

"They are outside playing with Dagan. Either Agee or Kirk is with them."

"Not truth," Grim growled, his whole demeanor changing as he spun around and stormed out the door he'd just entered.

"Not truth?" Lisa asked following. "What do you mean 'not truth'?"

Grim ignored her as he roared. "Agee! Kirk! To me!"

"Sire?" The two were quickly there.

"Where are my daughters?" Grim demanded.

"The Princesses?" They looked at him in confusion. "They are in the cottage with the Queen. We escorted them inside personally."

"They went out the back door to play with Dagan," Lisa told them, reaching up to grip Grim's arm. "I told them to take one of you with them when they went to find him."

At her words, two of her most trusted Elite Guard paled. "We never saw them, Majesty. Truth."

"*Find them!*" Grim roared just as the screech of an enraged Raptor filled the air.

∞ ∞ ∞ ∞ ∞

Dal, Eero, and Lalo looked up in horror and disbelief as a Raptor, in full attack mood, swooped down at them. Terrified, they abandoned their assault on Carly, Miki, and Dagan, and ran into the woods believing they would be safe there.

Grim raced up the path he knew his daughters had taken by the size of their small footprints. He forced away the memory of the last time he'd run on a path like this, to find his Lisa beaten and nearly abused. This time wouldn't be the same though. It couldn't be. His girls were too young, too precious.

As he rounded a bend, three bodies collided with him, each bouncing off him, flying to the side. Looking down, he saw three of his first-year trainees.

"Dal. Eero. Lalo. What are you doing here? Have you seen the Princesses?" he demanded.

"J... just exploring, King Grim," Dal stuttered, still frantically looking back the way they'd come.

"Princesses?" Lalo stammered.

"Yes, they were headed this way."

"M...meadow," Eero pointed up the path. "But they must be dead by now. There is a crazed Raptor there. It just attacked."

Grim's roar shook the trees as he raced up the path, praying to the Goddess he was in time.

∞ ∞ ∞ ∞ ∞

"Oh, Prince," Carly walked up to the giant bird that was now standing between them and the path the trainees had taken. "Thank you for helping us."

"Yeah, Prince," Miki said getting up from the ground. "They were bad males, but Dagan isn't." She helped the dirty and bruised Dagan up. "You remember Dagan, don't you? You met him in our garden."

Prince lowered his head, cocking it to the side as he stared at Dagan, his violet gaze seeming to take in every part of him then gave the slightest of nods. When sounds of running feet were suddenly heard, he spun around, spreading out his wings protectively to conceal the three of them behind him.

∞ ∞ ∞ ∞ ∞

Grim stormed into the meadow, his sword drawn just as the Raptor turned. Its wings were spread wide, and its deadly beak was snapping in warning. Grim took it all in, in a moment, including the fact that Carly, Miki, and Dagan were standing behind it.

Slowly sheathing his sword, Grim moved across the meadow, and Prince lowered his wings in the presence of the King, allowing him to pass. Grim dropped to his knees so he could carefully inspect each of his daughters, taking in the small scrapes and dirty coverings but finding no real harm. The same couldn't be said for Dagan.

"There it is!" Dal exclaimed. "Kill it before it attacks us again!"

"Prince didn't attack *you*," Carly exclaimed. "*You* attacked Dagan, and you would have attacked us too if Prince hadn't stopped you!"

"You lie!" Dal accused hotly.

"You dare accuse *my* daughter of telling an untruth?" Grim demanded quietly, slowly rising to face Dal.

"I..." Dal's mind raced. "She is confused. It was the idiot, the unfit one that was attacking them. We," he gestured to himself, Eero, and Lalo, "stopped him."

"Yet we found you running away."

"Only because of the Raptor," Dal claimed. "We had no way of fighting it off."

"So you chose to save yourselves instead of protecting two females?"

"I..."

Grim turned his back on the male and looked to Dagan. Going down on one knee before the unique male he'd grown fond of, he took in the darkening bruise along his jaw, the split lip, and torn shirt.

"Tell me truth, Dagan," he said gently. "What happened here?"

"I come here because I like it. It pretty," Dagan told Grim quietly. "The sun," he pointed up at the sky, "makes the ground sparkle." He pointed to where there was still some snow and Grim saw it did sparkle under Luda's sun. "It gives me ideas."

"I can see why," Grim agreed patiently. "But what happened today?"

"Like I say, I like it here, but not when they come." He peeked over Grim's shoulder at Dal, Eero, and Lalo, then quickly looked back to Grim.

"Why? What do they do?"

"They tease Dagan," he told them quietly, but everyone was able to hear. "Call me unfit, even though Dagan a good boy. They push me down. Hit me. Today they say they end me since my manno didn't." Dagan's split lip was trembling by the time he finished.

"He lies!" Dal yelled, but no one believed him.

Grim ignored Dal as he struggled to keep the rage out of his voice. He knew Dagan didn't react to it well. "You are not unfit, Dagan. You are a blessing from the Goddess, and your manno knew that from the first breath you took."

"Truth?" Dagan asked, his eyes pleading with Grim's that it was truth.

"The King of Luda doesn't speak untruths, Dagan."

And despite the split lip, Dagan's face broke out into a brilliant smile as he said, "That is truth."

Rising, Grim turned his gaze, pinning Dal and his friends as he bit out. "Kirk."

"Yes, sire," Kirk was immediately before him.

"You will take two guards and personally escort those three back to Luanda where they will be placed in containment cells until their mannos come and collect them. *If* they come to collect them." He watched all three pale.

"With pleasure, sire," Kirk replied then spinning on his heel escorted the three away.

"I'm glad they're gone, Manno." Grim looked down to find Miki looking up at him as she wrapped her arms around his leg.

"They will never harm you again, little one."

"They didn't hurt me, thanks to Dagan and Prince," she told him.

"Yeah, Prince scared them off before they could hurt us," Carly said, wrapping herself around his other leg, "but they did hurt Dagan."

"Hadar will heal him," Grim reassured her.

Grim looked at the creature that was still standing protectively between them and the remaining guards. He'd never heard tales of a real one doing such a thing. Only in the barely remembered myths that told of how the Great Raptor had once been the companion of a God. A God whose name only the stars knew now, and that this God had charged the Raptor with protecting those he deemed worthy when the God couldn't.

Those ancient myths couldn't be truth... could they?

"I thank you, Prince." Grim found himself using the name his daughters had given the bird. "For protecting those I hold precious when I wasn't able to."

The Raptor looked at the King of Luda for a moment, seeming to recognize that the King was just as deadly as it was when it came to protecting those under his care. Slowly, Prince turned his head and plucked out one of its long, jet-black feathers. When it took a step forward, Grim instinctively stiffened, even as he reached out to take the feather. But Prince dropped his head and instead offered the feather to Carly.

"For me?" Carly asked, her little voice full of wonder and when Prince nodded, she reached out to take it. "Thank you, Prince. I'll make sure to always take care of it."

Prince then looked at Miki, who gazed hopefully from Carly's feather to him. But instead of selecting a second feather, Prince gently nudged her tiny hand that was still resting on her manno's leg.

"What do you want, Prince?" Miki asked, reaching out to touch his regal head.

"Careful, Miki," Grim growled quietly, not liking the dangerous creature so close to his tiny daughter.

"But why, Manno?" Miki asked looking up at him. "Prince would never hurt me."

That's when Prince struck, embedding his razor sharp beak into the tender flesh of her tiny hand between her thumb and index finger.

Her shocked cry had Grim swinging his daughters out of harm's way, but before he could draw his sword, the Raptor was gone.

"Miki, are you alright?" Grim was once again on his knee, his hands trembling as he carefully tried to open the hand Miki had clenched to her chest, surprised to see that no blood was flowing down it.

"I... I think so," she told him. "Prince just surprised me."

"Let me see," he murmured gently.

"It doesn't hurt," she said, opening her hand so he could see it.

And there in his Miki's little hand, staring back at him, was the Eye of the Raptor.

∞ ∞ ∞ ∞ ∞

"What does it mean, Grim?" Lisa asked later that night after the girls were asleep. They had brought Dagan back to Luanda and Hadar had healed every bruise, and every cut, while all the Earth females had come to check on him. Dagan had won every one of their hearts with his gentle way and ready smile. He had left for home happier than Lisa had ever seen the special male.

Hadar had also checked Miki's hand, but there had been nothing for him to heal. No bruise, no blood, and no puncture wound. There was only a faint violet spot in the palm of her hand. He had tried to remove it with every portable repair unit in House Luanda, but every last one of them found nothing to remove.

Now they were in their sleeping chamber, the House was quiet, and there was a roaring fire before them as Grim handed her a small glass of wine.

Grim sighed heavily as he sat down next to her on the couch. "The Raptor's feather has been given since the earliest of recorded times. Although I've never heard of a Raptor itself gifting one."

"What do you mean?"

"The finding of a Raptor's feather is a rare thing. No one knows why so finding one is an honor."

"Why?"

"Because it is believed that only true protectors are allowed to find and wear them."

"True protectors?"

"Yes, those that protect, serve, and watch over those that can't do it for themselves. The way the Great Raptor does for the people of Luda."

"But Carly is just a child."

"And yet she came to the aid of Dagan. We have both seen how protective she is of Miki... and of you. She is a worthy recipient of the Raptor's feather."

"And Miki's hand?"

"The Eye of the Raptor." Grim's voice was much more hushed this time, almost pensive.

"Why do you say it that way?" Lisa demanded, her stomach clenching.

"The Eye of the Raptor. Lisa..."

"Yes? What about it?"

"Few have ever heard of it, and even fewer know what its gift is."

"Just what did that damn bird do to my baby?!!" she demanded, setting her wine aside.

"He gave her the ability to sense the evil and darkness that is Daco."

"What?!!"

"I know of only one other that has ever been gifted the Eye. It is said that while he saved many from Daco's clutches, it came at a terrible cost."

"What cost?"

"That is not known."

"Goddess, Grim. What are we going to do?"

"Nothing."

"What do you mean *nothing*?!!"

"Calm, my Lisa," Grim told her, gently framing her face with his large hands. "First, because there is nothing we can do and second, what I've just told you is a myth. It doesn't mean it is truth."

"But..."

"No," he gently admonished her. "You said yourself that Carly was always your little Warrior, was looking out for Miki and you, even before she came here."

"This is truth," Lisa nodded calming slightly.

"As for Miki, she *never* liked Luuken."

"*No one* liked Luuken," Lisa muttered.

"Truth. So you see, it is nothing she didn't already have before. Do not place so much belief in myths that have been spoken of for thousands of years."

"I suppose you're right," she said, relaxing back into his arms, taking the glass he held out to her again.

"Of course I am. I am the King of Luda." His comment got him exactly the reaction he was hoping for. His love gave a little huff of disbelief and rolled her beautiful eyes at him, but the last bits of worry and tension left her body, and she snuggled down deeper into his embrace. "Now let us enjoy the fire and maybe... if you aren't too tired, we could light one ourselves later."

"Oh, I think that can be arranged."

Epilogue

Several days later...

"My Queen still doubts that you are the right male for this task, Warrior Ull," Grim said looking across his desk at the Warrior standing there.

"With all due respect to your Queen, King Grim, she knows nothing about me so is in no position to judge my abilities."

"It is not your abilities she doubts, Warrior Ull," Grim told him. "It is your attitude since the Joining Ceremony. She and Lady Abby speak regularly. As do I and Lord Ynyr."

"They feel they have the right to criticize the assistance I gave them?" Ull questioned, his rose-colored skin darkening in anger. "Assistance they requested? To you?!!"

"Neither complained of your help, Warrior Ull. In fact, Lord Ynyr repeatedly praised you, stating that without you, it would have taken him a great deal longer to get House Jamison in order. It is because of that, Wray chose you for this."

"Then what was their complaint?" It should have eased Ull's temper, hearing that his brother acknowledged and appreciated everything he had done for him. But it didn't. Instead, it made him angrier. Why would it take the word of a *third* male, Lord or not, for him a *first* male, to be given this honor? It didn't make sense, but there was a great deal that wasn't making sense to him lately.

"That you seemed... unlike yourself since the Joining Ceremony."

"They are wrong."

"I hope so because your brother warriors' futures, and perhaps that of our entire Empire, depend on the outcome of this mission." Grim let that hang for a moment then reached out to hand Ull a memory crystal. "This is the transmission Lisa recorded for her friend, Trisha. You must find her, convince her to view it, and convince her to help."

"She will," Ull growled. "My vow."

∞ ∞ ∞ ∞ ∞

"Rebecca," Grim and Ull walked to where his Lisa and a group were standing next to the shuttles. One would take Ull to the Searcher, while the other would take General Rayner, Jennifer, and Rebecca to the General's ship, the Defender. It had been decided that Rebecca would travel on the Kaliszian ship as Jennifer had become progressively sicker in the mornings. "I have informed Lord Callen that you will be on Pontus."

"What?" Rebecca asked sharper than she had intended. "Why would you do that?"

"Because Vesta is the closest Tornian planet to Pontus, and is where others will be told you are should any inquire. Its Lord needed to be informed."

"Oh, of course."

"Lord Callen is also the one that will be returning you to Luda when the time comes. Should you need him before that, for anything, contact him with this." Grim handed her a small, palm-sized object. "It is secure and will not allow others to know where you are. That is important, Rebecca. Should it become known that we have allowed a compatible female to leave our Empire..."

"Yeah, yeah, yeah. I understand. So my cover is that I'm meeting with Lord Callen."

"Cover?"

"Reason for going," she explained.

"That would be truth then."

"Rebecca!" Every head turned to see Miki running across the grounds toward them, weaving her way through the bodies that separated her from her goal. Three guards were trying to keep up.

"Miki?" Rebecca knelt down as Miki reached her. "What's wrong?"

"You can't leave!" Miki told her breathlessly. "Not without these."

Rebecca's frown turned into a smile as she opened the bag Miki had shoved into her hands. "You brought me cookies?"

"Yeah, Mommy used to always make them for us when we went on a long trip, so I thought you should have some too."

"Thank you, Miki." Rebecca hugged the little girl. "I'm sure these will make my trip much more enjoyable."

Miki smiled then backed away from Rebecca until she ran into her manno's legs. Or at least she thought they were her manno's, but when she looked up, she found herself looking into the dark eyes of Warrior Ull. Eyes that, for a moment, were darker than they should be.

"Miki," Grim lifted her up into his arms. "What have we told you about running from your guards?" That had her gaze moving to him instead of where it had remained locked on Ull's.

"But I wasn't, Manno," she told him earnestly. "Vow. I just didn't want Rebecca to leave without her cookies."

Grim released a heavy sigh realizing this was a subject he would be addressing again and again as his little one grew.

"King Grim," General Rayner's lips twitched as he nodded slightly, "and Princess Miki. It is time for us to depart."

"Safe travels, General Rayner. Remember you are carrying treasured cargo," Grim looked to Rebecca.

"No one knows that better than I do, King Grim," Treyvon told him, but his gaze went to his Jennifer.

"Bye, Uncle Treyvon. Bye, Aunt Jennifer. Bye, Rebecca." Miki waved as they walked away and Lisa didn't bother to correct her that technically she was wrong. Her girls had eagerly accepted Treyvon and Jen into the family, and if this was the way they wanted to express it, then she'd let them.

∞ ∞ ∞ ∞ ∞

Ull tipped his head to the side slightly, watching the group say their goodbyes and felt nothing. No, that wasn't truth, he felt something... something dark.

'We shouldn't be working with the Kaliszians.' The thought insidiously whispered through his mind. *'They are weak. We can take what they have,*

take what Earth has. That would better serve our brother warriors. It would make them see who the worthy and fit one was in his family.'

Ull didn't know where these thoughts were coming from, but they made sense. There was no guarantee his mission to Earth would succeed. After all, what did the Emperor know? He was allowing a *female* to influence his decisions, just like the King of Luda was, as was the Supreme Commander of Kaliszian Defenses. It made them weak. Females were only ever meant for one thing. All females.

His gaze went to the little one in the King's arms and was surprised to find her staring unflinchingly back at him.

"Beware the darkness that speaks to you." Miki's words while quiet were spoken in a voice much older, wiser, and more powerful than hers could ever be. "It knows where you are most vulnerable when you are at your weakest. It then lies to you with the truth, making you believe and do things you never otherwise would. Terrible things. Beware the darkness, Warrior Ull."

"Miki," Grim growled looking down at his youngest in shock. Her hand, the one with the Raptor's Eye, gripped his neck and for a moment he felt such power radiating from it that he thought it would burn him, and her eyes seemed to glow.

"What, Manno?" she asked, her voice once again full of innocence, her touch was cool, and her eyes were the beautiful amber of her mother's.

Grim's gaze went to Ull to demand what had just happened, only to find the Warrior closing the hatch of his shuttle.

"I should have brought cookies for Warrior Ull," Miki said, watching as the shuttle flew away. "He's not very happy."

"That is truth, little one." Grim's concerned gaze remained on the shuttle.

"Maybe Trisha's cookies will make him happy. They're the best."

∞ ∞ ∞ ∞ ∞

Michelle has always loved to read, and writing is just a natural extension of this for her. Growing up, she loved to extend the stories of books she'd read just to see where the characters went. Happily married for over twenty-five years, she is the proud mother of two grown children and a grandmother of one perfect little girl. You can reach her at m.k.eidem@live.com or her website at www.mkeidem.com. She'd love to hear your comments.

∞ ∞ ∞ ∞ ∞